A catalogue record for this book is available from the British Library

Published by Ladybird Books Ltd
A subsidiary of the Penguin Group
A Pearson Company
LADYBIRD and the device of a Ladybird are trademarks of Ladybird Books Ltd Loughborough Leicestershire UK

Disney's

THE LITTLE MERMAID

Ladybird

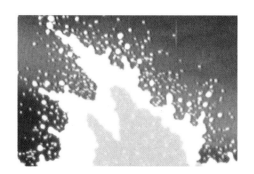

It was going to be a great concert, in the depths of the ocean. All the undersea world was invited – the lobsters, the rainbow coloured fish, even the winkles. The only one who hadn't been invited was Ursula the Sea Witch.

The Royal Musical Director, Sebastian the crab, stood beside the music stand, elegant in his red costume. The young mermaids were playing among the seaweed, passing the time happily as they waited for the concert to begin.

Any minute now King Triton, ruler of their undersea world, would arrive. And then this very special evening could get under way.

Trumpets sounded. "His Majesty!" a sea horse announced. Here came the King of the Seas, trident in hand, in his chariot drawn by three dolphins. Hearing the fanfare, the young mermaids stopped playing and rushed out of the seaweed to watch.

Sebastian the crab came forward and bowed to the king. Then he tapped his baton on the music stand. Now the concert could start.

"Just a minute," interrupted King Triton. He had looked all round the audience in the Great Hall of the Palace and was annoyed to find his youngest daughter wasn't there. "Where has Ariel got to? She's supposed to be singing a solo."

Ariel had forgotten all about the concert. She was far away, with her friend Flounder. They were exploring the wreck of a sunken ship – a ship that had once been part of the wonderful world of humans.

"Oh, Flounder, look at all these things that used to belong to humans," said Ariel. She held up a strangely shaped object. "What's this?"

"How should I know?" said Flounder. "I'm only a fish."

"I know who'll know," said Ariel. "Let's go and find Scuttle." Scuttle the seagull always knew everything…

Ariel was eager to show Scuttle her new treasure.

He looked at it carefully, turning it this way and that. "It's a dinglehopper," he said seriously. "Humans use it to comb their hair, like this." He started to hum cheerfully as he showed Ariel what he meant.

"Music!" gasped Ariel, suddenly remembering. "The concert! Father will kill me!" And she dived straight into the water, leaving the others looking at each other.

Triton was in a right royal rage. "There you are," he thundered when Ariel arrived. "Where have you been? Everyone's waiting for you."

"I'm sorry, Father," said Ariel. "I just forgot, I'm afraid."

"I'm not listening to excuses," said the king. "I hope you haven't been to the top of the sea! You know I've told you never to go there. Those terrible humans might see you. They might want to make you into fried fish. Have you thought about that?"

"They aren't dangerous!"

"How do you know? My little one..."

"I'm not little! I'm sixteen years old, Father!"

"Don't speak to me like that! As long as you live in this ocean, you will obey me. If I hear that you have been on the surface, you will be punished."

"Sir, children are impossible these days. They do as they like," said Sebastian as soon as Ariel had gone away.

The king turned to him. "Was I *too* severe with her?" he asked.

"Not at all, sir. Ariel needs watching," said Sebastian.

Triton brightened. "That's a good idea. And you are just the crab to do it. From now on, you can keep an eye on Ariel."

That didn't please Sebastian at all – he had been looking forward to spending some time on his music.

Not far away, in the shadows, were two eels, Flotsam and Jetsam – the Sea Witch's spies. They hadn't missed one word of that little chat...

Where was Ariel? Sebastian searched for her all over the place. He found her at last in her secret cave, surrounded by her treasures.

They were poor, broken things, most of them. But every single one spoke to Ariel of the world above that she dreamed of so often. How she envied the people who had used them!

She was talking excitedly to Flounder. "Look how wonderful they are. How can people who make such beautiful things be bad? I would really love to know them." She swung round. "What's that?"

It was Sebastian – he had just tripped and fallen with a tremendous crash.

"Sebastian! What are you doing here?"

"Oh, I was just passing," said Sebastian.

"You're not going to tell the king where you found us, are you?" asked Flounder.

"Please don't tell him," begged Ariel. She knew her father would be furious.

So Sebastian promised not to tell.

At that moment, a shadow crossed the entrance to the cave. *A ship!* thought Ariel and she swam to the surface.

On board, sailors were dancing and clapping their hands in time to the music of an accordion. Laughter and singing rose into the night. The sky flashed with fireworks of all the colours of the rainbow.

Ariel gazed and gazed, spellbound. She had seen many ships before, but never as close as this! Sebastian and Flounder watched with her. So did Scuttle, who had flown down to join them.

"The best is still to come," said Scuttle. "Prince Eric's on board, and everyone is going to sing Happy Birthday to him."

Ariel wanted to see everything properly. Although Sebastian tried to stop her, she swam right up to the ship. Now she could see what was happening.

She could see Max the dog. She could see Grimsby, the prince's treasurer. And she could see Prince Eric! He had just opened his birthday present from the sailors – a statue of himself.

Ariel kept her eyes on the prince – she wanted to see if he liked the statue. Behind her, black clouds began to race towards them.

Then the storm broke. The wind blew harder and harder, and the waves grew bigger and bigger. Huge drops of rain began to fall. Thunder crashed and lightning lit up the sky.

Prince Eric was at the wheel of the ship, trying to keep it on course. But the wind and waves were too much for him. The ship was blown onto a rock and the sailors took to the lifeboats.

Before the prince could join them, the worst happened. Lightning struck the ship and it burst into flames. The prince was flung into the sea.

"Eric!" cried Ariel, horrified. She hurried to his rescue as fast as she could. She mustn't let anything happen to a prince from the wonderful world of humans!

Eric sank through the waves, and Ariel followed him down, her heart beating rapidly. He would die if she didn't catch up with him quickly.

Suddenly she lost sight of him. She searched to and fro, to and fro, getting more and more worried. Still no sign of the prince.

Ariel went up to the surface again to try once more. She dived again and again beneath the salty waves, and at last she saw him. His eyes were closed and his arms trailed through the water.

Ariel took the prince in her arms and pulled him to the shore. Now the sky was clear, and waves gently lapped the beach. The storm was over. And Ariel had saved the prince from drowning.

But *had* she saved him? Eric lay very still on the golden sand with his eyes tight shut, and Ariel didn't know what to do.

"It's all right, he isn't dead," Scuttle told Ariel. "He's breathing."

Ariel began to sing softly. After a moment, as she sang, she saw Eric's eyelids flutter. Then, just as he opened his eyes, Ariel quickly dived back into the sea.

Only Flotsam and Jetsam knew all that had happened.

In the depths of the ocean, Ariel was humming a little tune. "He loves me… a little… a lot… Oh, Sebastian, I'm sure Prince Eric loves me," she said happily. "I want to go back to him," she went on. "I wonder if Scuttle knows where my prince lives?"

Sebastian wasn't nearly so happy. He knew if King Triton found out how badly he had looked after Ariel, there would be real trouble. And if he learned that his daughter had fallen in love with a human, the king would be in a right royal rage – again!

Ariel's heart was full of happiness, and she wouldn't even listen to Sebastian's advice.

Meanwhile, down in her lair, the Sea Witch now knew everything from her two spies. Her evil laugh rang out again and again as she made her wicked plans.

"There you are, Ursula," she told herself. "That little mermaid who dreams of a prince charming is going to fall straight into my hands. And that will put Triton in my power. He will have to come to me to save his daughter."

Just what was the Sea Witch going to do?

Sebastian was a very worried crab when he went into the throne room to meet the king. He didn't know how he was going to tell Triton what had happened.

The king's first words were, "Have you been taking good care of Ariel?"

Sebastian turned even redder than usual. "Sir," he said, "I'm afraid Ariel has fallen in love with a human being."

Triton seemed to grow taller. "Where is she?" he asked.

"Your majesty, I think I know," stammered Sebastian.

Ariel had gone back to her cave of treasures, the faithful Flounder trailing behind her. There she found a great surprise – Prince Eric's statue! Flounder had rescued it for her. But before she had time to look at it properly, her father arrived.

"Ariel, we don't even live in the same world as humans," he said. "Can't you understand that?"

Ariel tried to tell him how she felt, but it was no use.

White with rage, the king raised his trident and struck the prince's statue. It broke into a thousand pieces.

It wasn't long before the Sea Witch heard from her eels about Triton's anger – and Ariel's unhappiness.

"Bring her to me!" ordered the Sea Witch. "Ariel can go back to her prince – but she will have to pay the price."

Flotsam and Jetsam went to Ariel and invited her to go with them to the Sea Witch's lair, because she would help her. Ariel was a little frightened, but she obeyed.

Ursula was admiring her new shellfish necklace in a mirror when Ariel arrived. The little mermaid was horrified to see how ugly the Sea Witch was. And how cruel she looked!

"So, you love this prince," said Ursula, looking down at the little mermaid. "And you would like to become human. You are a brave girl, and I am going to help your dreams come true."

"Can – can you do that for me?" asked Ariel.

"Yes – thanks to me you will become human for three days. And if the prince kisses you before sunset on the third day, you will stay human. If he doesn't, you will turn into a mermaid again, and belong to me for ever!"

"Oh, thank you, that's wonderful," said Ariel.

"Just a moment, though. In exchange, you must give me your voice."

"My voice?"

"That's right, your voice," said Ursula. "Now, do we have a deal or not? If we do, sign this contract."

Ariel thought hard. Did she really want to go through with this? But if she had legs, she could go and find her handsome prince. She signed the contract.

No sooner was it done than Ursula ordered her to sing. As Ariel's voice rose, pure and beautiful, the Sea Witch crouched in front of her cauldron, chanting strange spells.

Then an evil smelling mist filled the room, and fingers seemed to grip Ariel's throat. Her voice left her, swallowed up by the strange shellfish necklace that Ursula was wearing.

Ariel left the Sea Witch's cave wondering just what she had done. Then she thought of her prince, and felt happier. Now she had legs, she would go and find him.

But Ariel couldn't swim nearly so quickly as before. So Flounder and Sebastian helped her to get to the surface.

Once she was on the beach, that was different. Ariel's long legs jumped happily over the waves, and danced along the sand. Scuttle flew overhead, whistling cheerfully as he watched her.

Since the day of the storm Eric had often thought of the girl who had sung to him so beautifully.

That morning, he couldn't believe his eyes. There was a girl strolling along the beach – surely she was the one?

He went up to her and asked, "Do you remember me?"

Ariel could only nod in reply.

When he found she couldn't speak, Eric realised she could not be the one. But he felt sorry for her and led her back to the palace with him. Scuttle and Sebastian followed them.

At the palace, Ariel was given a wardrobe full of fine clothes, and all the food she could eat.

She loved everything she saw. Some of them she had seen before, when she had been collecting treasures from the human world in her cave.

She found one of these in the dining room, and she smiled when she saw it. It was a fork.

A dinglehopper! thought Ariel. *It's lucky Scuttle told me what it's used for. How silly I would look trying to eat with it.*

And picking up the fork, she combed her hair with it.

The prince's treasurer, Grimsby, came into the room at that moment, and was very surprised indeed.

It wasn't long before the whole palace was talking about the beautiful silent girl who combed her hair with a fork.

Next morning, Eric took Ariel out for a ride. He wanted to show her his kingdom.

In the afternoon, he took her out in a boat on a quiet lake. And wherever they went, there were anxious whispers – among the leaves, among the reeds, in the water.

"Has he kissed her yet?" asked a heron.

"No," sighed Sebastian. "Not yet."

Desperate to help his friend, Sebastian walked to and fro, to and fro, thinking. If Prince Eric didn't kiss her soon, Ariel would belong for ever to that evil Sea Witch.

"I know, Scuttle," he said suddenly. "Music – that's what we need. Sing, Scuttle!" But Scuttle wasn't the best singer in the world, and Sebastian soon told him to stop.

Then everyone sang together, "Kiss her... kiss her..."

Ariel looked up at Eric and smiled. He leaned forward to kiss her... nearer... nearer...

But as their lips were about to meet – the boat turned over!

Flotsam and Jetsam had been busy again!

Ariel woke bright and early the next morning. The castle was buzzing with excitement – the prince was getting married. Ariel was overjoyed when she heard the news and she ran to look for Eric. But the first thing she saw when she went downstairs was Prince Eric with his arm round a girl with dark hair.

Eric was saying to his treasurer, "Grimsby, I'd like you to meet my future wife, Vanessa. She sings like an angel. We're getting married this afternoon."

"I hope you'll both be very happy," bowed Grimsby.

No one noticed Ariel as she ran away in despair.

The wedding ship with Prince Eric and Vanessa on board left that afternoon.

Scuttle flew out to see what he could see and heard a beautiful voice raised in song. It sounded just like Ariel. But how could it be?

He swooped down and saw – Ursula the Sea Witch! He blinked and looked again, and it was Vanessa, the prince's bride. He looked once more and saw Vanessa looking at herself in a mirror. But it was the Sea Witch looking back at her, an evil smile on her face!

Scuttle knew he had to find Ariel and tell her about Ursula's wicked plan!

As the ship grew smaller in the distance, Ariel sat on the quay and sobbed her heart out. Sebastian tried to comfort her, but he knew it was no good.

Suddenly Scuttle flew down to tell them what had happened. "It's Ursula," he stammered. "The prince's bride is really the Sea Witch. And she's singing to him in Ariel's voice! I've just seen her looking at herself in the mirror."

"We must stop the wedding!" said Sebastian.

But stopping the wedding was going to be easier said than done.

Scuttle hurried to ask his friends to help.

"Ursula has put a spell on Eric! Come on, we can't let her marry the prince. Quick, the ceremony is about to start."

All the sea birds raced towards the ship. Ariel followed them, but very slowly, because she couldn't swim properly with legs.

Flounder brought her a barrel and said, "Hang on to this, and I'll pull you along."

On deck, the Sea Witch was attacked from all sides. Her wedding dress was torn and spoiled. Terrified, she tried to escape from the sea gulls' sharp beaks.

The birds went on pecking Ursula. The plan was to stop her saying the final "Yes" that would tie her for ever to Eric.

It was the third day of the spell, and the sun had begun to go down. Soon it would be too late for Ariel and her prince.

Ariel's friends knew what would happen when the sun had gone. Driven by despair, they began to fight even harder. The Sea Witch was in real trouble.

Suddenly her shellfish necklace flew off and broke on the deck. A golden cloud came out of it, and set Ariel's voice free.

The evil spell was broken.

"Eric… my prince," cried Ariel.

Eric knew her immediately and came towards her. "It was you who rescued me, that day when I nearly died," he said, smiling in wonder.

He took her in his arms, to give her a gentle kiss.

But the last rays of sunlight had gone. He was too late.

Ursula was watching them, her eyes gleaming. She gave a shriek of triumph that rose to the stars and echoed all round.

She had won and Ariel knew she now belonged to Ursula!

The prince watched, horrified, as Ursula grew into a hideous monster. She grew bigger and bigger, with enormous tentacles stretching from side to side of the ship.

Then she seized Ariel and threw her overboard. The little mermaid floated on the sea foam, then sank slowly beneath the waves.

"Farewell, farewell, my true bride," murmured Eric with a sad heart. He was sure he would never see Ariel again.

Scuttle's friends the sea birds had told King Triton what was happening. He rushed to the Sea Witch's lair and thundered, "Set my daughter free!"

"Your daughter?" laughed Ursula. "She belongs to *me* now. She signed a contract. But I will do a deal with you – her freedom for your power." She paused. "Give me your crown and your trident, and Ariel goes free. Well?"

Without further thought, Triton agreed. And at that instant, his name took the place of Ariel's name at the foot of the contract. Also at that very moment, the King of the Seas was turned into a horrible slug.

Ursula was proud to be Queen of the Seas. She waved Triton's trident around, pleased. Then she began to grow once more, into a gigantic terrible monster.

Her powerful roar shook the earth, so that even the birds flew as far away as possible. From her eyes shone a cruel beam. When she started to swim, her enormous arms raised waves as high as mountains.

Never had anyone seen such a terrifying sight. From now on, nothing and no one could stand against her.

Suddenly Prince Eric appeared, ready to give his life for his little mermaid.

He caught up a harpoon and threw it with a mighty heave at the Sea Witch. She ducked and it missed her, but she dropped Triton's trident as she did so.

Ariel grabbed it and pointed it at Flotsam and Jetsam. The trident's powerful beam hit the Sea Witch's eels and killed them instantly.

Ursula was so furious that she was foaming at the mouth with rage. She grabbed the trident back from Ariel, and went to attack Eric.

"You can't escape me now!" she roared.

All sorts of shipwrecks had come to the surface during the storm, and Eric swam towards the deck of one of them. Once on the deck of the ship he held grimly onto the wheel trying to hold it steady as the ship creaked and groaned through the water.

Then as the ship rose on the crest of a wave, the prince came face to face with his enemy. The Sea Witch had become huge beyond belief, and she was churning up the sea into a violent whirlpool.

She glowered down at him from a great height, holding the magic trident in her hand. As she came nearer and nearer, Ursula became bigger and bigger. At last she seemed to fill both the ocean and the sky.

Waving the trident triumphantly, the Sea Witch came slowly towards the prince. But Eric was ready for her, gripping the wheel firmly.

He steered straight for Ursula – and the ship hit her right in the middle of her huge body.

A fearful roar echoed through the night. All who heard it trembled with horror.

The Sea Witch had met her end!

Now that Ursula had gone, all those she had held in her power went back to their own shapes. Triton was King of the Seas once more.

"Thank you, thank you," Ariel said over and over again to all her friends. "Without you, I would have been lost. I will never forget you."

Scuttle, Flounder, Sebastian – they had all helped. And here they were to share in her happiness.

Nearby, Prince Eric smiled at her tenderly.

Her father himself had shown Ariel how much he loved her. He had raised his magic trident – and given her human legs for ever. Only Ariel knew how much it had cost him to do that.

From now on, the youngest daughter of the King of the Seas would no longer live near him, at the bottom of the sea.

A few days later, Eric and Ariel were married on board the wedding ship. King Triton proudly watched over them from the sea – and sent them a rainbow.

"I think they're going to live happily ever after," said Scuttle as they kissed tenderly.

And just for once, he was right!